D A N   Y A C C A R I N O

DOUG UNPLUGS ON THE FARM

ALFRED A. KNOPF   NEW YORK

This is Doug.
He's a robot.

Doug and his parents are going to visit the grandbots!

“Everyone plug in!” said Dad.

“We’ll be driving through farm country,” said Mom. “You can learn all about farms on the way.”

Doug’s parents wanted him to be the smartest robot ever.

Doug learned bushels of facts about farm things:

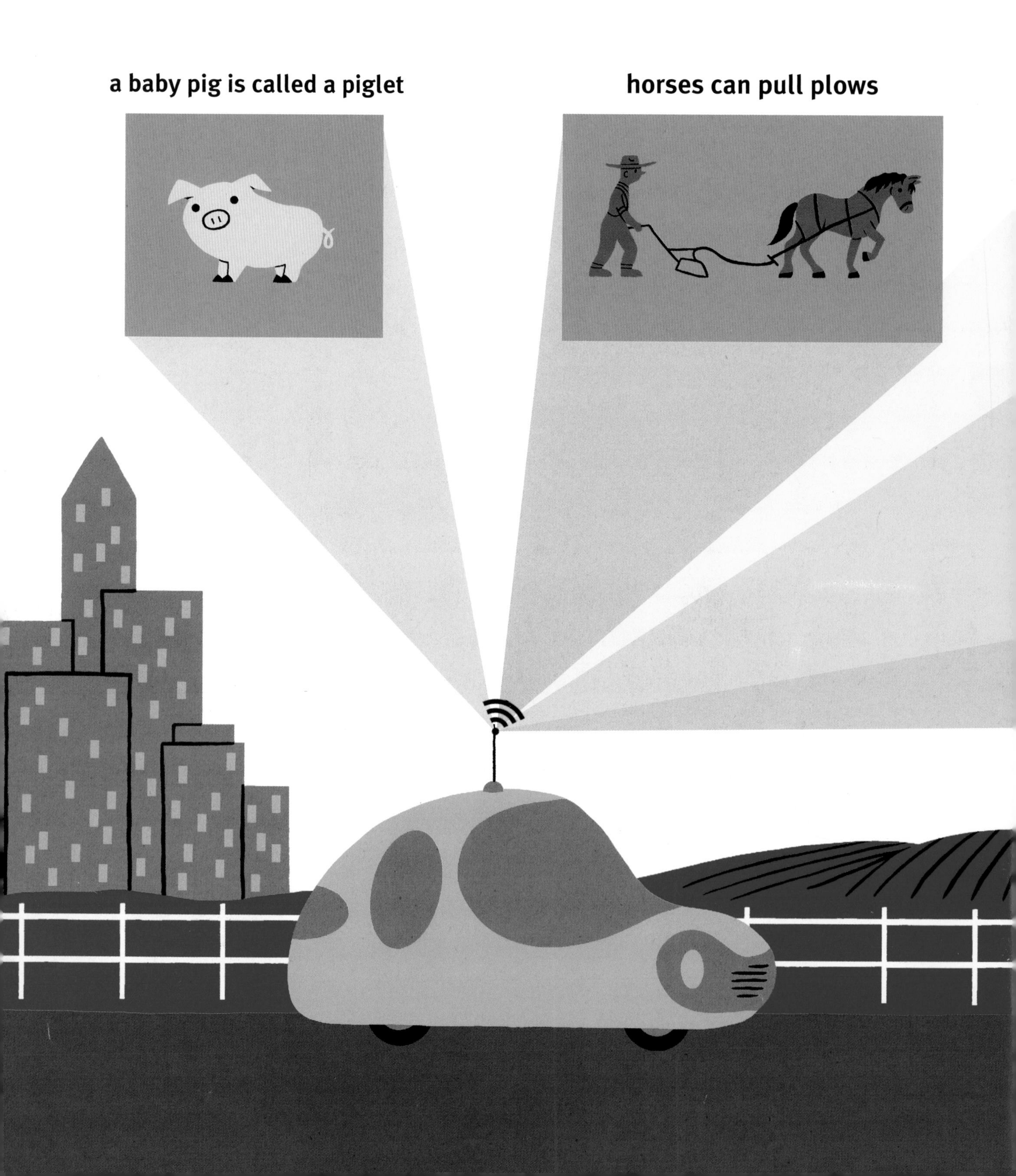

cows need to be milked every day

chickens lay eggs

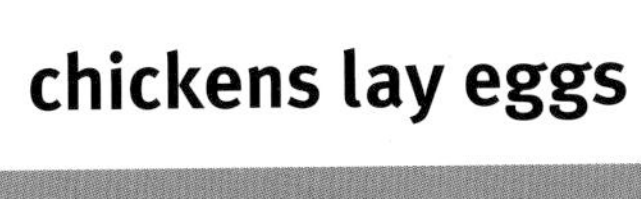

apples grow on trees

sheep tend to follow each other

He was just learning about how sheepdogs can herd sheep when suddenly . . .

A whole flock of sheep ran into the road!

And their car went into a ditch! And worse—the whole family came unplugged!

"Oh dear," said Dad.

"Oh my," said Mom.

"Oh boy!" said Doug.

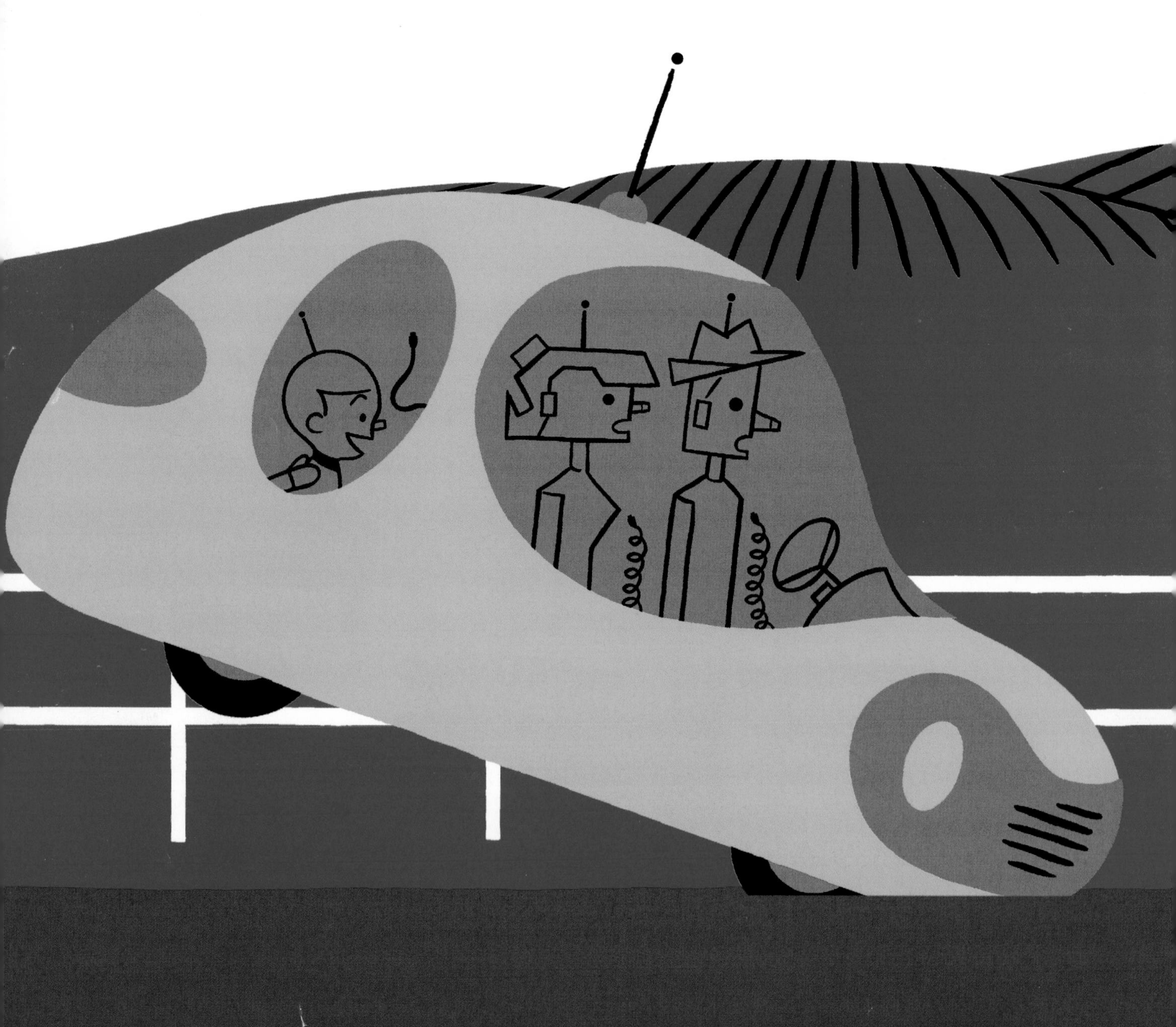

N
E
W
S

Doug could see that the farm girl needed help.

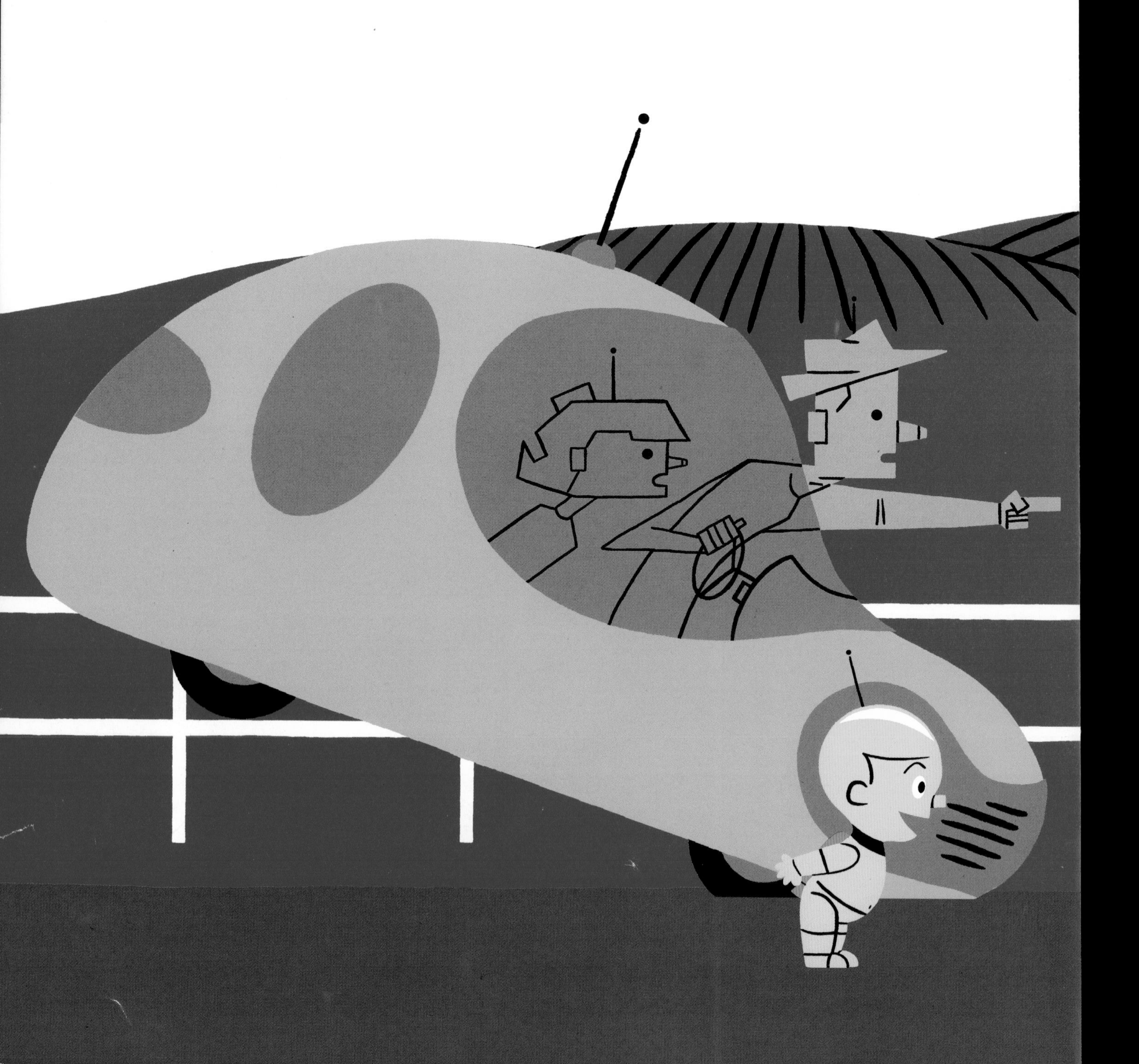

N
E
W
S

And so he made like a sheepdog, and together they rounded up those sheep.

“Thank you!” said the farm girl. “Want to help with the rest of my chores?” she asked.

Doug did!

“Don’t go far,” said his mom.

N
W
E
S

Doug knew that milk came from cows, but he actually got to milk one! And he learned that a cow's tongue felt rough.

They got hay from the barn—prickly!

And picked apples from a tree—delicious!

The horse thought both the hay *and* the apples were delicious.

He scattered corn for the ducks.

And Doug learned that baby ducklings liked to follow him.

The farm girl fetched water from a deep, dark well,

and Doug learned how thirsty—and smelly!—pigs can be.

When he gathered eggs from the henhouse,

Doug learned that roosters can be bossy.

The rooster even chased the cat onto the roof of the barn! Luckily, Doug could fly up to get her.

Doug could see for miles from the top of the barn. He could see his parents—and that their car was still stuck in a ditch.

He could also see a tractor.

Doug knew that tractors pulled heavy things—maybe it could pull their car out of the ditch?

Dang! The tractor was out of gas. But Doug had another idea.

A horse! Of course! The horse had their car back on the road in no time.

N
E
W
S

Doug and his parents thanked the farm girl, and her horse, and got back in their car.

"Everyone plug in," said Dad.

But Doug stayed *unplugged*. He thought about all the ways he'd helped out on the farm. And all the stories he'd have for his grandbots.

“I picked it myself,” Doug told them.

And they thought he was the smartest little robot ever.

For Eliza

THIS IS A BORZOI BOOK PUBLISHED BY ALFRED A. KNOPF
 Published in the United States by Alfred A. Knopf, an imprint of Random House Children's Books, a division of Random House LLC, a Penguin Random House Company, New York.
Knopf, Borzoi Books, and the colophon are registered trademarks of Random House LLC.

Visit us on the Web! randomhouse.com/kids
Educators and librarians, for a variety of teaching tools,
visit us at RHTeachersLibrarians.com

Library of Congress Cataloging-in-Publication Data
Yaccarino, Dan.
Doug unplugs on the farm / Dan Yaccarino.
p. cm.
Summary: Doug the robot takes a hands-on approach to learning about farm life when the family car gets stuck in a ditch on the way to visit the grandbots.
ISBN 978-0-385-75328-9 (trade) — ISBN 978-0-385-75329-6 (lib. bdg.)
— ISBN 978-0-385-75330-2 (ebook)
[1. Robots—Fiction. 2. Farm life—Fiction.] I. Title.
PZ7.Y125Dq 2014
[E]—dc23
2013039893

The illustrations in this book were created with brush and ink on vellum and Adobe Photoshop.

MANUFACTURED IN MALAYSIA
July 2014 10 9 8 7 6 5 4 3 2 1 First Edition
Random House Children's Books supports the First Amendment and celebrates the right to read.